MW00973822

The Squirmy Wormy
Written by
Amy M. Fathers

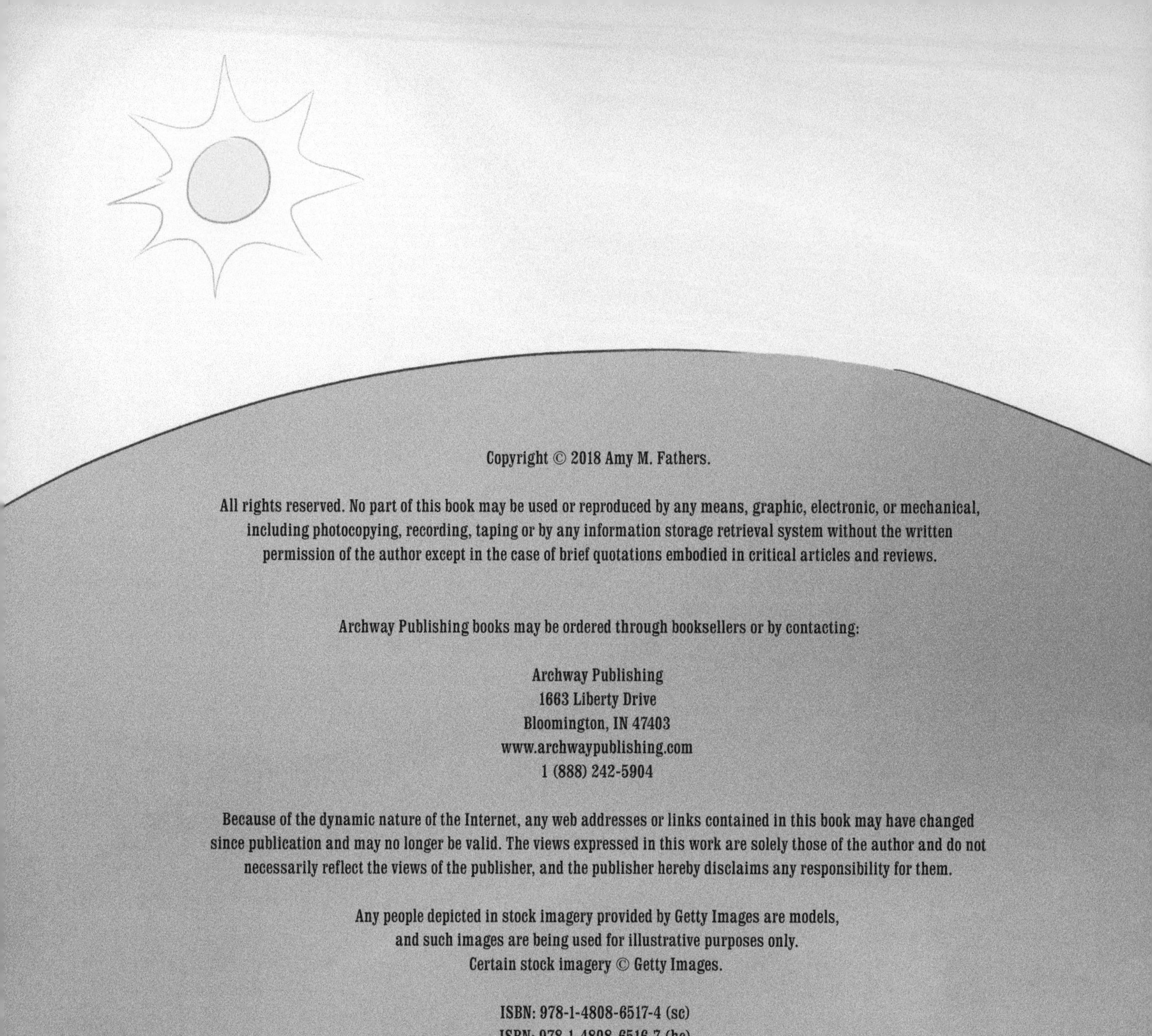

Archway Publishing books may be ordered through booksellers or by contacting:

Archway Publishing
1663 Liberty Drive
Bloomington, IN 47403
www.archwaypublishing.com
1 (888) 242-5904

ISBN: 978-1-4808-6517-4 (sc)
ISBN: 978-1-4808-6516-7 (hc)
ISBN: 978-1-4808-6518-1 (e)

Print information available on the last page.

Archway Publishing rev. date: 7/31/2018

For Peter

You will always be my squirmy little wormy. I love you to pieces.

Acknowledgements

This book would not have been possible without the tremendous and unwavering support from my husband, John, my parents, Paul and Terry, and of course the biggest inspiration of all, my son, Peter.

There once was a little wormy.
All of his friends called him Squirmy.

He loved to dig holes in the dirt
And wore an apple on his shirt.

Squirmy lived in the front of a big, old house
High up on a hill with his friend Squeak the Mouse.

Andy the Ant was also part of the squad
When he wasn't down deep and stuck in the sod.

The crew lived in a town called Apple Creek,
And when it rained hard the roofs would all leak.

But when the wind blew the houses would stand.
They were all made of bricks and were quite grand.

Every day Squirmy would look for some fun,
And Squeak would join when not on the run.

Up and down the hill the two would go,
But when the winter came there was snow.

Then the spring would arrive, and the flowers would sprout,
And there was no reason for Squirmy, Squeak, or Andy to pout.

On would come summer and time for the beach
And peaches on the trees that they could all reach.

Around the corner was fall with leaves orange and red,
And it was time for Squirmy to rest his little head.

The sun was about to set and welcome the night.
The three best friends were tucked in and all was just right.

The stars were shining. The sky was clear.
It was a perfect night for all to share.

About the Author

Amy Marie Fathers grew up in Belmont, Massachusetts, where she spent her childhood enjoying summers in the sand, winter on skis, fall in apple orchards, and spring mostly under umbrellas. Amy has been in the public relations industry for nearly twenty years, working with clients in the financial and professional services industries. She spent two years in Bangalore, India, and she traveled extensively throughout that country and elsewhere in Asia and the Middle East. In her free time, Amy volunteers at a local animal shelter and trains for her next marathon! She currently lives in Manhasset, New York, with her husband, John, son, Peter, dog, Sula, and cat, Mathey.

______________________'s Pictures

______________________'s Pictures

________________________'s Pictures

______________________'s Pictures

______________________'s Pictures

CPSIA information can be obtained
at www.ICGtesting.com
Printed in the USA
BVHW02*1745020918
526315BV00006B/9/P